Wilfried Kriese
BRUNO´S FREE FLIGHT TO KENYA
Life behind hotel walls A narrative

Mauer Verlag
Wilfried Kriese
72108 Rottenburg a/N
Cover Layout: Wilfried Kriese
Edition Wilfried Kriese 2017
First edition 2001
All rights reserved
ISBN: 9783868124958

www.mauerverlag.de
www.wilfried-kriese.de

Inhalt

Chapter 1

1 HERE

There's nothing much to say about Bruno. What is there to be told about Bruno anyway? Except that he is something different, just like all the other people, too, who just live their lives the way they are supposed to. Or why should a creature dwell on earth if not to live, possibly to die? No, let's not talk about dying, otherwise one might not feel like living anymore, if one begins by looking for a meaning of life that could plausibly explain why there is so much life and death around on earth?

Bruno is in his late thirties, 5 feet 80, of medium weight, that is: he has the slight tendency of a round belly and a flattened bottom. Bruno is proud of not having to wear glasses like so many of his age, instead, he's beginning to cultivate an inferiority complex due to his slowly vanishing hair. He doesn't wear suits, but neat trousers nonetheless and plain shirts with no tie and ironed pants, but nobody sees that anyway.
So much for a rough description before going into detail.

Bruno has also the tendency of riding his mountain-bike in his cycle shorts every now and then, and right now he is riding homewards. He feels as happy as a man can whose civil service career has ended. He's proud of his bicycle in particular, it's the latest and best among all bicycles. It has 36 gears, forward and backward shock absorbers, a comfortable saddle, an ultra light weight frame (whatever ultra means, but ultra light weight anyway), superb tyres with specially developed brakes.
So he's on his way to the new housing estate where about 8 years ago, he and his wife built a small, detached, self-contained house, which however lacks a balcony, since Bruno is not a civil servant of the executive class but only of the clerical class. If he was merely the kind of civil servant a caretaker is, he would at

best have a terrace-house or rather a small flat in the city. But if he was a civil servant or an employee whose career ended 5 years before Brunos professional advancement, he could have afforded even a semi-detached house with a garden and two rose bushes.

Bruno is riding past the most diverse houses, then rows and rows of terraced houses appear, located only 300 yards away from his proud home. He´s glad that he has achieved more than his father. It´s not that Bruno, the solitary child, thinks bad of his father or even looks down on him, no, he certainly doesn´t, even if he wanted, he couldn´t, God or whoever bless him, since he has to be grateful to his father for so many things after all, just like many a Christian has to be grateful to God: 1. life, 2. genes and 3. inheritance and a fat dowry for the marriage ten years ago and the Original Sin, since his father was a soldier during the Third Reich, but no ordinary soldier, but... no, it would be too much to take for Bruno, if this was decribed in greater detail here; it would certainly be different, had the War been won... Yes, all of this Bruno inherited from his father, although he had been just an ordinary blue-collar worker. And that´s enough for Bruno to be what he is today: a faithful, wealthy voter for the party with the capital C, where conservative is being written as large as Christian. And this exactly is the reason for Bruno´s happiness, as he has just been at the election party celebrating his party´s victory together with partisans; well, maybe it´s not his party, since he is just a small civil servant as is well-known, and not a high civil servant, or an industrial magnate, or a bank chairman, or a mafia chief, or even all in one.

He considers the Christian´s Party´s victory to be a rescue for his occupational group in particular from all alternatives. For people like Bruno are sure that the word alternative has no place in the working place or in private life, since it will only disturb the calm rhythm of everyday life, where every suggestion of change is seen as an act of rebellion.

Bruno turns off for the entrance of his sweet home. There he parks his bicycle. Across from him his neighbour waves in front of his little terrace house with two rose bushes.
Before a conversation can come up, Bruno grabs the opportunity and walks up to the main door and closes it behind him quickly. He takes a deep breath. It´s not that Bruno has anything against his neighbours, they are honest and diligent citizens. Besides, he has as little against his neighbours as against lawyers and judges.
But still, one thing cannot be seperated from the other.

Red Sonja welcomes Bruno brushing against his feet as always. Red Sonja is the Holbeins´ cat, that is Bruno´s wife and son´s. Red Sonja isn´t just some cat, no, she is a thoroughbred Persian cat with a family tree and awarded ancestors.
Bruno cannot recall how many times he has stumbled over the snow-white cat with black paws because of her permanent brushing against his feet purring. Maybe it is the case of a purely domestic cat that has never caught a glimpse of freedom having its own special kind of revenge. For even a cat needs gratification.

In the living room, the TV is running.
„Hello, darling, you´re just in time for the Elephant´s Round!“, his wife Margot welcomes him.
„Dad, will you say goodnight to me?“, a voice shouts down from the nursery through the staircase.
„Is the Elephant´s Round already running?“
„No, you still have two minutes.“

When Margot has finished the words „minutes", Bruno is already standing at Sebastian´s bedside. He is 6 years old and is a child like every other, or maybe, almost like every other child. For he has an IQ of 111,11 and is being promoted in every way possible. So, in spite of his biting fingernails and his occasional need for uppers or downers and his full schedule, he is as advanced as a second form pupil for somebody who is just entering school, and there´s one thing the parents are sure of, Sebastian won´t end up as a blue-collar worker one day.

Bruno says goodnight to the boy, kisses his forehead hastily, then puts out the light and closes the bedroom door.
„Dad, leave the door open a bit, it´s so dark!"
Dad obeys.

Bruno is sitting on his TV couch, just in time for the Elephant´s Round: the party leaders´ post-election discussion programme. After 30 minutes of accusations, self -praise, acknowledgements to the voters and assistants and political statements on the level of political election campaign leaflets and top candidate bills of the parties represented in Parliament, the broadcast is over and the TV chanel continues its programme.
Margot presses the remote control and sound and vision disappear from the screen. Bruno fetches two wine-glasses from the house-bar and fills them up to the rim with white wine.

Bruno´s wife is the same age as her husband, a bit shorter than him, dark blond hair of medium length and she wears glasses, much to Bruno´s dislike, and this is exactly the reason why she refuses contact lenses.
Margot is a secretary, but she is no ordinary typist, but 1. a personal assistant, 2. an undismissible public employee and 3. she´s sitting in the anteroom of an institute director who distinguishes

himself particularly by being punctual, strict, correct, extremely conservative and by not getting tired of mentioning his degrees of Doctor of Philosophy, Science, Letters, Law and what not over and over again. At this point, the question may be raised what kinds of compromise a grey-haired man in his mid-fifties must have accepted in his younger years in order to be later capable of boasting four degrees, especially without any known scientific work worth mentioning. But this is a different issue, since Bruno is the main character after all and nobody else, not even Bruno´s wife who is so self-sufficient and self-confident that she has been asking herself for several years what the difference between husband and wife may be actually. Therefore, it might be interesting to get to know more about Margot.

Since the time she became a personal assistant, she has been conservative and only for this reason does she vote for the same party like her husband. However, she used to vote for a different one before, but that was then and today isn´t yesterday and certainly not the day before. Compromise just has to be accepted in everyday life if a woman wants to make it as a personal assistant of a Doctor in Philosophy, Science, Letters, Law etc.

She runs the household the way somebody is supposed to whose husband runs away from it whenever he gets the chance - squeaky clean: the proper state for an orderly German household. It´s not that Margot was proud to be German, no, certainly not, but just like Bruno, she attaches great importance to their Polish charwoman´s thorough cleaning of everything and to her storing everything in its right place. For, after all, there are German traditions that have to be maintained.

Apart from work and housework, Margot has to take care of her son´s upbringing, although his father considers this to be as much a part of life as a cuckoo does. She didn´t take long to convince Bruno to register Sebastian first in kindergarden, then in day nursery, and now even in day school. For why should these institutions exist if one wouldn't make use of them in spite of high charges, even if one is a single person with low earnings? And if somebody just cannot afford these exorbitant monthly fees, then they'll just have to do without children and especially women who first marry, then bring children into the world and eventually get divorced, certainly don't have any reason to complain.

For all of this is not the proper thing to do!

They both agree.

So Margot and Bruno sit in front of their now half-emptied glasses and yet they hardly have uttered a word. The only thing she said was:

„Thank God we still have our old chancellor, what would have become of us if the Social Party had made it, together with the Alternatives? Even more foreigners and thus even more unemployed people.“

It's not that the Holbeins had anything against foreigners, no, they even employ a Polish charwoman themselves, who 1.is more diligent than her German predecessor, 2. is more punctual and 3. doesn't even demand a third of a badly paid German charwoman's salary.

Well, anyway, the only thing Bruno replies is: „I agree, darling.“

And that's the end of the conversation. For, after all, two people who have been married for 10 years and who have known one another for an equally long time have little to say the other hasn't heard at least 1,001 times before.

Bruno gets lost in his thoughts.

Everthing used to be different. Father used to wear the trousers and never would it have crossed mother's mind to put them on, or even think about them, unless it was about washing and ironing them.

Mother was the perfect housewife who, though she used to moan every now and then, never seriously complained. Although she had just one child, the idea of earning her own money would have never occurred to mother.

Bruno takes a swallow of wine. Then he turns off these thoughts. There is however still a lot to say about his father.

Bruno's father used to be conservative, too, and after the war he voted for the Christian Party, just like his son does today. Delegates, ministers, party officials of all categories, of his kind, used to be in power, who preferred to talk about the present and the future than about the right-wing past. Today, these politicians, along with their voters, have become extinct and their ghosts are now trying to come alive again through their grandchildren and also their great-grandchildren. Some of these ghosts have floated towards the National Party where they are now being voted into the here and now.

Father used to earn his money all his life as a machine operator in the factory, which he hated. Therefore, he made it plain to Bruno from his early childhood onwards, that he should learn something better than his father later, a profession where 1. one won't break one's back, 2. one won't get dirty and 3. one will nevertheless receive an ample salary so that one doesn't have to go short of pants.

Bruno isn't and wasn't a hell of a rebel and minded father's wisdom of life, and so Bruno eventually made it as a doctor in biology in the civil servant career of the clerical class.

„I´m going to bed, Bruno!"
He opens his eyes slowly and replies: „I was just thinking about that, too."

In the bedroom, they undress. At this point, it should be noted that there are a great deal of bedtime strories to report of couples that have been living together as long as the Holbeins, involving real good, red-hot sex before sleeping, but in this particular case, well...

Their eyes have barely closed and sleep has barely crept in, when the alarm clock sends out an increasingly loud buzzing signal.
Immediately after waking up from sleep, Bruno deals with the daily round. A brief toilet, a brief breakfast and a quick coffee. At work, he intensifies his breakfast with a coffee and an extended newspaper break followed by a sandwich break. But first he´s got to get to his work place. By foot, 3 miles are too much for him, which is why he sometimes prefers the bicycle, since everybody should show some concern for the environment after all, even if it´s nothing but show. He might as well go by bus or tram, but that doesn´t fit his status and would make him face too vehemently the normal working people and ordinary life. For, after all, he´s isn´t just a civil servant like a patrol officer or a janitor, but a doctor and a superior.
Today, just like about always, Bruno prefers the car. However, he doesn´t drive an ordinary middle class car, but a BMW of medium category, he couldn´t afford a larger BMW or a showy Mercedes, since he´s not a professor or a doctor of philosophy or a doctor in philosophy, medicine etc.

On his way to work, Bruno always passes by apartment blocks where mostly blue-collar workers with low income live. Tthe council flats are located a little further away. In his thoughts there's rarely any tolerance of welfare recipients, who all too readily dodge honest and hard work such as emptying refuse bins, for example. For - this is Bruno's conviction - there has to be somebody who does this very important work, which is why Bruno doesn't look down on refuse bins, however, there's one thing he's dead sure of, he would never work at the refuse disposal service!

Bruno holds these workers in great esteem, since he was a righteous worker's child himself and therefore he knows what it means to be a worker, he thinks he knows anyway. For Bruno was a worker's child during the times of the German economic miracle and not today where there are nearly 5 million unemployed and 2.5 million welfare recipients and countless short-timers.

The remainder of his way to work is as meaningless as a blocked-up toilet, the flushing of which had been forgotten too often.

Show me your office and I'll tell you who you are.

Bruno's office is at the end of the corridor facing the Gents and the Ladies. He's long got used to the flushing.

The office of the superior, a professor and doctor, is located at the other side behind a secretary's office with seating facilities for visitors and lots of windows.

Bruno's office has just one window and at most 15 square yards and his paper work is done by himself.

Bruno, too, is a superior, but the word „superior" can mean different things. Bruno is superior to 8 charwomen, 3 janitors and the institute shopworkers. Somebody who is a professor and a doctor, for instance, would never be satisfied with having these underlings. Apart from Bruno, two other colleages, who are doctors, supervise Bruno's underlings. Most of the superiors have further titles, which have been invented in the course of decades in order to make one seem important. Oh, and these three have three superiors on their part who in turn are being supervised by three superiors who... which eventually leads us to politics that calls the shots; this makes it plain why everything is as it is in civil service.

One thing´s for certain, however. Bruno is as dutiful and in accord with regulations, as a truly faithful Christian who follows the Ten Commandments, so that it takes a lot to imagine Bruno endangering his position by acting autonomously; this is what makes him so popular with his superiors.

Due to the risk of getting bored, the remainder of Bruno´s work routine will be skipped.

At exactly 15:30, Bruno prepares for closing-time and at exactly 16:00 he´s sitting in his car.
At 16:18, Bruno is standing in front of his door. Just as he´s inserting the key into the lock, he startles, as if something as impossible as a ghost had passed by him. His wife has opened the door with a jolt. With a loud and nervous voice she says: „Bruno, Bruno," she´s breathing heavily. Bruno replies worriedly: „What´s wrong? Has anything happened?" - „No, nothing, or, I mean, y-yes!" - „So what happened?" - „Guess!"
Thinking hard, Bruno takes off his shoes and his jacket at the wardrobe and thinking even harder, he walks into the living-room where he sits down. But he just can´t think of anything that could be so exciting as to explain Margot´s behaviour, which, after all, is violating all of their off-time norms.
Bruno has to swallow hard now. Because the last time she was that excited was when she told him that she was two months pregnant, and from then onwards, all their instances of excitement have been determined by everyday situations. But

Margot pregnant? No, that's impossible. For 1. she takes the pill, 2. her work is sacred to her and 3. what could have made her pregnant anyway?

Bruno answers: „I don't know, tell me!"

She is holding a bottle of sparkling wine and two glasses in her hands. Now Bruno is assured that she is certainly not pregnant, because when she was pregnant with Sebastian, she didn't even eat chocolates filled with brandy or a piece of cherry cake, let alone pure alcohol.

The cork pops out. The glasses foam over. Margot puts a glass in her increasingly irritated husband's hand, raises hers and says: „Cheers!" Then she empties it with one big gulp. Maybe his mother-in-law has died, it occurs to him, but no, if this was the case, Margot would certainly be drinking something stronger than sparkling wine.

Then she bursts out: „We have won a journey abroad at this state lottery „A PLACE IN THE SUN" worth 10,000 Marks and now guess where we'll fly?"

„Oh, I think I've done enough guessing now, come on."

„To Kenya! Two weeks, full board in a four-star hotel. Isn't that great? Sebastian is beside himself with joy."

A hesitating nod on Bruno's part.

Bruno is as happy about it as about a rainy holiday.

„Kenya! Good God, Kenya, that's pretty deep in the middle of Africa!" he thinks. At once, horror visions of asylum seekers pop up in his mind, people who just want to have an easy time in Germany at the diligent taxpayer's expense.

This much is certain, Bruno will have an easy time in Kenya, too, but only as a chance tourist for only 2 weeks, and not as a plague. After all, Africa is a beautiful continent, even if living isn't that wonderful here and there, but then again, his father didn't become an asylum seeker in the Third Reich either, just because there were some problems, no, he stayed and he lended a hand and kept up the best he could.

Since Bruno´s marriage, the Holbeins have been on the Italian Adriatic coast for their holidays. Once, they had to choose another beach hotel because their regular hotel was being restored. Every year they make one or two trips into mainland Italy, so Bruno ist quite sure that he knows Italy quite well since he has seen nearly all the tourist attractions.

So Bruno has still to come to terms with the prize, although the real reason for his pool wasn´t exactly charity for people in need, but the hope of getting rich instantly. For very few people make donations for free, since one wants value for money, even if it´s only the hope of getting rich.

Bruno stops his brooding, he stands up and clinks glasses with his wife hesitantly and says: „Well, cheers then!"

For the last two weeks, the Holbeins have been sent flight tickets, travel information and glossy brochures about Kenya and its safaris.

After reading the brochures, Bruno manages to find the thought of Kenya more and more appealing. Among others, he read this about Kenya´s history: To experience a Kenyan sunrise evokes the feeling of experiencing the world in its first morning. Its vastness presents the country in its primary pureness.... about 40.000 years ago, the first immigrants settled in the north. Theses ancestors were nomads, warriors, craftsmen and peasants. Then more groups wandered south along the Nile, until the Massai, too, arrived in the last millenium.

Furthermore, Bruno read about colonial rule in the 12th century by the Shirazi immigrants and about the Portuguese discoverer Vasco da Gama (1648) and the related wars that went on until 1698.

Then there were passages about Africa´s division in the 1880s, the important economic foothold and the railway´s conquest that provoked a series of wars with the natives. Before 1901, Mombasa used the be the most important town, then Nairobi was declared the capital.

There were also things to read about Kenya´s development from 1952 to the present day, about Jomo Kenyatta´s designation as the first president. He was elected on December 12, 1963 when Kenya gained independence as a republic. On August 22, 1978, the president died and only a few hours later the vice president Daniel Arap Moi was sworn in. Then Bruno learned some figures and dates about Kenya in the glossy brochures. Size: 224.6 square miles; about 28 million inhabitants; system of government: democratic republic; the first and the current president; capital: Nairobi, most important port: Mombasa; highest mountain: Mt. Kenya, 5.686 yards above sea level.

A warm and sunny climate during the greatest part of the year is guaranteed.

Then he was also informed about the most important words in the local language, like, for instance, „can you tell me the way to the hotel? I would like a bottle of coke, hello, coffee, eat, lion, giraffe...“

And finally he read that everything there is cheap. Then there were great praises of the fauna and the safaris, the white beaches with their palm-trees and miraculous de luxe hotels and of vaccinations that were part of the travel conditions. All of this was enough to dazzle Bruno more and more and to put him in a state of euphoria about the coming holdays in Kenya.

Bruno was given a description of Kenya the way nowadays a child is given a description of God.

Oh, by the way, low salaries, unemployment, economic misery and poverty, as well as destruction of the environment by tourism and foreign investors, famines, political prosecution and torture... are not mentioned in the information brochures.
They have no business to be in Bruno´s head, what would be their use in there anyway since Bruno´s everyday life is hard enough after all, and you mustn´t let reality spoil your holidays.

Ten weeks have past since then and two weeks still to endure before the departure.
Mother and child are awaiting the holidays with a tension like in a cigarette advertisement. Even Bruno´s everyday routine seems to last eternally. The working day has barely crept away when the evening turns into a fast, living computer whose programs are busy calculating, analysing and executing all of the holiday preperations.

The Holbeins bear all kinds of vaccinations necessary for tropical regions, regardless of the impact on their health. Masses of pills against malaria are prescribed as well, and finally a medicine chest is added which would outshine any pharmacy salesman´s assortment.
Sun protection lotion with a factor of 0-25 is purchased.
Then the camera equipment is brought up to date in a way which would make any Japanese green with envy. And last but not least: „Leisure time is reading time“, literature must be bought, whatever it may be. Like in any everyday situation, Bruno doesn´t rely on his own judgement but follows those of others, of critics. Some books are literally torn to pieces in media reviews bordering on book burning. It´s quite interesting that critics

often don´t even have the most unimportant journalistic awards to show and didn´t achieve more during their professional career of 10-20 years than many a civil servant of the clerical class did.

All right, a critic has to let off steam, too, in some way.

Anyway, Bruno decides to buy a 500-page tome of a bestselling author which has received rave reviews. The novel, by the way, was published by a company with an enormous marketing budget.

It´s April 13, three months after the state lottery fortune had struck. The Holbeins got through the motorway safely and now the car is standing on the airport car park protected by three alarm systems.

Before the Kenya adventure can begin, the airport adventure has to be defeated first. Bruno gets the impression that with all the civil servants in plain clothes and in uniforms, the adventure without risk is a chaotic, huge and hectic airport.

After waiting for two hours they check in. The luggage is weighed and dragged through the customs. Everything except for the waiting time is going the quick German way.

Then there is some more waiting in the departure lounge, along with the other 250 patient passengers.

Bruno pulls a newspaper out of his hand luggage and there it is in over-sized bold letters with a huge photograph of the catastrophe: „123 DEAD IN PLANE CRASH". Fear is creeping over him.

„My God," Bruno thinks, „and me sitting here!!!"

Pearls of sweat are gathering on his forehead. It occurs to him that it probably would have been better to have forgone the journey, for what´s the use of a free flight won in the state lottery if the plane will crash down? He should have gone to his familiar beach hotel on the Adriatic coast by car instead. It´s better than flying, you don´t fall from the sky.

But the fact that in Germany alone about 9,000 (nine thousand) children, adolescents, women and men get killed in traffic per annum and that 500,000 (five hundred thousand) are injured - and these are only the registered cases, doesn´t occur to Bruno. That would be too much for his conservative, blind mind.

The flight to Mombasa is announced finally. Bruno and his family are among the very first who may board the plane, first class. Then the second-class passengers are on and at the end those of the third class. Bruno, however, would never have booked third-class tickets, for he´s more than third-class, after all.

The interior of the airplane amazes Sebastian the way a spaceship would. With all the technical data and measures, there´s a lot to investigate for a mind with an IQ of 111,11.

Bruno´s anxiety reaches its climax. With loud roaring, the plane is taking off now.

Shortly afterwards, it´s lunchtime. The passengers are served their meals, like battery hens. They have chicken with potato salad. It tastes just like McDonald´s.

After the meal, tax-free products are offered by attractive hostesses, so that not only the desire to buy is stimulated in some passengers. Then, it´s already time to sleep. The hostesses´ instructions before take-off about what to do if the plane should crash after all are crossing Bruno´s mind, then Bruno falls into an uneasy sleep.

Chapter 2

THERE

Shortly after the morning´s feeding of the passengers, the captain´s voice resounds: „Ladies and gentlemen, were are now aproaching Mombasa...“
Nervous anticipation...
After touch-down, Bruno takes a deep breath, „Phew!“, they landed safely.
Exiting the aircraft nearly takes his breath away. For the air is humid and warm to a degree only possible in the tropics. And, uh-oh, there are dark clouds gathering over the Mombasa sky. Then their way leads through the customs. Everything is moving as smoothly as in Frankfurt, though much more slowly.

Outside the airport, the luggage is stored under heavy sweating because the Holbeins are dressed the way they had been at home, which is as adequate as wearing a bathing-suit at the North Pole.
The shuttle bus pulls off. Several parts of the vehicle rattle here and there and the bus driver´s driving style almost makes one recall the forgotten art of praying. Instead of the brakes, only the klaxons are being applied on the uneven, narrow roads that are filled with oncoming traffic and speed is maintained constant. On their way, the passengers see Mombasa´s street-life. Bruno prefers closing his eyes at the first sight of the ghetto-like houses, or rather, at the first sight of the huts in danger of collapsing.
For the first time, Sebastian´s eyes behold the Kenyan children, who not only dream of wealth but of shoes, of shirts and of trousers with not that many holes in them, and of at least one good meal per day.
At last, Bruno can open his eyes again and, little wonder, Margot does as he does. For this is where the hotel accomodation area begins. The landscape is turning green and starts to blossom.

Tall palm-trees are rising up to the skies. Yes, this is the world most tourist dream of.

Finally, can you believe it, the hotel appears. They have reached their goal!

While Germany and Kenya used to be worlds apart some 50 or 60 years ago, today you need as much time to get here as a manned flight to the moon.

The first day passed quickly. And the fourth day has already begun. In the meantime, the Holbeins have checked out the surroundings and, most importantly, the mealtimes. There are four meals a day, breakfast, lunch, dinner and, apart from that, afternoon coffee or tea including sandwiches. The buffet's variety resembles a fool's paradise. Salads, pasta, rice, meat, fish and the most terrific African fruits - surrounded by the most delicious deserts - make for a healthy appetite. And not too far from all that food, there's HUNGER, not too far? We're not talking about a distance like the one from Germany to Kenya or Somalia, it ends just in front of the hotel walls. There are as many hungry mouths living there, as there are grains of rice in the hotel dining hall. But that doesn't affect Bruno and his family's, or most of the other guests' appetite. The buffet is so numbing that everybody stuffs themselves past all reason. As a consequence, there are diarrhoea pills for a second desert.

The hotel grounds are truly like an impossible dream for the natives. Unless they belong to the staff here. Room-boys, waiters, askaris (wardens), grouped in two hierarchical levels, together with a married Swiss couple, cater for heaven-like wellbeing of the European guests, who will have their holidays at any cost. A 3 persons' sojourn costs as much as an hotel employee will earn in 10-15 years, provided he's not the manager, and a bottle of wine is worth half a month´s salary. The staff make most of the guests feel like they were a three-tier wedding-cake. Thus, there are as many employees in the hotel as there are tourists.

Palm-trees are rising up to the skies over the white sunny beaches. Every now and then, the bathing and sun-mad tourists grow pale. For it is the beginning of the rainy season and around here there is either a rainy or a dry season, unlike Germany where there are as yet four relatively predictable seasons.
If there is rain in Kenya, European minds are stunned. Because only somebody who has experienced the Flood may think this kind of rain possible and nobody will be that old?

After breakfast, everybody runs to the beach. The Holbeins have discovered the Indian Ocean´s underwater world, along with countless other tourists. Equipped with diving goggles, snorkels and flippers they stomp into the Kenyan northern shore. Which means for the underworld: 1. Caution, snorkel-colonist are approaching, 2. enjoy your remaining time as long as you can, 3. say goodbye to existence.
Anemones, sea urchins and crustaceans are being trodden upon and the fish learn the meaning of panic and escape.
But before reaching the sea-shore, the beach boys have to be dodged first. They are natives selling everything from small wooden elephants, all kinds of souvenirs, to safaris and they are following the bathing-mad like a swarm of flies in order to make a deal.
These native merchants are often portrayed by the hotel managers as mafiosi who will only cheat you. Which Bruno believes, too. For in Germany, the opinion about black people isn´t that great after all. So the fact that the hotel charges up to three times more for a safari than the offerors at the beach is of no importance and Bruno is convinced that what the hotel manager couple

says about their powerful competitors are hard facts and this conviction is worth a lot of money. For, as the management rightly says, everybody will cheat you. What they do not say, however, is that some will cheat you less than others, and in this respect it´s better to let yourself be cheated by one of the beach boys than by the European hotel keepers.

The snorkeling tour is over. Bruno, Sebastian and Margot are still stunned by the fantastic underwater world (which has finally received the coup de grâce).

It is evening and the guests´ stomachs are digesting the four meals. And Sebastian is lying in bed. There he´s dreaming about Walt Disney´s „LION KING".
Bruno and Margot are, after settling in their relatively fastidious room, down at the evening dance.
There is no TV set in the room, a fact which the three haven´t come to terms with as yet. Some guests have allegedly departed ahead of schedule just because of that.

The evening dance features a local band. With electric guitars, bass, organ and drums, they provide the right mood. However, this kind of music has as little to do with original Kenyan music as German folk music has with the dying forest.
Between sets a 3 feet tall dark native with large feet enters the stage in a military uniform. He marches around while English military music is playing and the audience applauds, swiveling around a long truncheon while the music is beating time: TIP-TIP-TIP-TAP-TAP-TAP-TACK-TACK-TACK-TIP-TIP-TIP...
Then this soldier takes off his proud uniform and turns into a martial arts performer. With truncheons and kung-fu tricks he makes the audience rave.
Then the band plays on. Not far off, out of view, the soldier and

the three askuris are hiding in the dark laughing heartily about their performance and even more about the tourists.

If Bruno and the rest took a look at themselves, they would start to wonder more about their mentality than about the staff´s, whose most frequent word is „polepole" (slowly, slowly). Bruno is wondering anyway why every single member of the staff´s first and second name isn´t polepole. For there seems to be a competition going on here and the winner is the one who is the slowest of all.

After the second bottle of wine and meaningless conversations with their holiday acquaintances, Bruno and Margot go up to their room. Sebastian is sleeping tight and, now isn´t that something, there´s even a bedtime story...

Two days later, Bruno´s sunburn, which has been torturing him since the beginning of the holidays, is slowly disappearing. But Bruno doesn´t give a damn about the sunburn, he wants to get a tan, at any cost. He has underestimated the equator sun totally and this means pain, burning pain.

In order for his red skin to acquire the desired tan, the two-day safari to the Sava East and West Reservation, about 75 miles from Mombasa, is just right.

„Jambo," greets the native, black jeep-driver outside the hotel. Bruno, Margot and Sebastian and five other hotel-dwellers of all ages answer with a fivefold „Jambo, jambo, jambo, jambo, jambo!"

Jambo is Suaheli and means hello, or to be put it differently, it is the Suaheli word which comprises all kinds of greeting.

„Polepole!" the driver says as excitement arises among the Germans while storing their travel luggage.

Sebastian is more excited than he has been for a long time, because today is the day he may finally see the home of Walt Disney's „LION KING".

The chaos of excitement goes on, till the driver says „Polepole, hakuna matata!" and stores the luggage himself and has the passengers climb in.

„Hakuna matata" is the most frequently used native expression after „jambo" and „polepole" and means „no problem."

Often the native population is just amazed at what the tourists consider to be problems, and just say: „Hakuna matata." The reason probably is that to the natives, who have experienced hunger and misery, the foreigners' problems must almost seem like blessings.

When the natives talk to each other, one can hear a mixture between English, Suaheli and bits and pieces of other languages. That's why, as an outsider, one can always understand a couple of words and then guess the meaning of the rest.

Now the trip begins. Off we go to the safari, that is: we go travelling, because in Suaheli, which is the official language in Kenya apart from English, Safari means travel. But this is something the travel agency adventurer does not know and therefore thinks it means animals, wilderness and adventure.

Along the streets, the people live in utter misery. They can nonetheless spare a smile for the strangers, who they wave their hands at. In spite of poverty the people can feel happiness in a natural way. Then some small and medium-sized villages appear which partly consist of 10-200 huts. Huts? For German conditions any chicken shack is a pleasant apartment in comparison. Even Bruno has to notice that the people here don't live from hand to mouth but from little finger to small hollow tooth.

Here begins the region which makes every tourist´s heart beat faster. For everything is turning green and more and more tropically shaped trees stretch out across the landscape. And to the passengers´ great relief, the reality of the Kenyan street-life disappears. So, after a four-hour trip, which was pleasant and cool thanks to the open windows, they have finally arrived at the Sava East National Park. Here they quickly check in at the Hilton Lodge. The lodge is constructed over round concrete posts that look like tree trunks and is designed in the style of Tarzan´s tree-house. Apart from that, everything in it is of course custom-made luxury convenience that hasn´t anything to do with the wide country.

The first excursion starts off on fixed routes with guide posts reminiscent of German trails. Sebastian looks around in amazement with his eyes and his mouth wide open. For the first time he experiences the Kenyan fauna, that is to say, the remainder of it. For the big game hunters, along with poachers, who were always after hunting trophies the way tourists are after carved timber souvenirs today, did a great job.
Up until now, the boy knew the tropical fauna only from Walt Disney´s „THE LION KING", in spite of his IQ of 111, 11. Now he realizes that Walt Disney has been taking him for a fool. For 1. the lions and all the other animals aren´t as brightly coloured as in the film, 2. the animals and the nature are so wild and dangerous that Sebastian has to be careful not to wet himself and 3. the animals don´t grin and talk as in „THE LION KING". Little zebras and herds of antelopes and water buffalo next to a single giraffe, as well as an iguana, make the cameras grow hot. The minute a species has been photographed, it loses its attraction. Because for Bruno and the rest the animals are simply motifs for the albums at home. For you have to be able to prove that you have seen all of the tourist attractions, after all. The

thought that it might be interesting to watch the animals a little longer doesn´t cross the passengers´ minds.

The day is over, and many an animal has been immortalized on photographs. In the lodge there´s a good deal of gorging and boozing. Then it´s off to bed. The room offers everything that a travel agency tourist in Kenya can be offered. It´s large, has a shower with hot water and a toilet. Simply put, the room doesn´t even offer a hint of a real tree-house.

The next morning at 8 a.m. all the luggage is stored in the jeep and the journey heads for the Massai village. The Massai are an old Kenyan tribe that has been known for its pride and honour, at least that´s what the travel brochure says. So, of course, everybody is curious, especially Sebastian, as he will finally see real „Indians". The ride stretches over long roads of red earth. A comparatively light tropical rain starts to fall. It is worth noting that around here there may be heavy rain at a temperature of just 5-10°C and only 100 (one hundred) kilometres away there is a tropical heat that withers any vital harvest. But this is of no importance for the Hobeins. They just get upset about the rain, that is central to the survival of plants, animals and humans. After all, they booked „A PLACE IN THE SUN" in Kenya, didn´t they?
Finally, after an hour has passed, the village is becoming increasingly distinct to the passengers, so distinct that they see Kenya as it was 100 years ago. What a shock, now the rain is good for something in the end. For at the sight of the round huts made of dry cow-pats and the primary, or in Bruno´s eyes, primitive and insanitary Kenyan conditions, the weather turns out to be their rescue.
„We´re not getting out!" everybody cries out in unison. The eight passengers seem like petrified. The first few Massai approach

hopping about with friendly faces and swarms of May-flies behind them that would make every swarm of bees appear as small as a mosquito.

Within short time, the jeep is surrounded by about 20 Massai. Some of them look at the vehicle the way Sebastian would look at a spaceship. The Massai invite Bruno and the rest to take a walk around the village.

„No-no-no!" everybody cries out in unison.

One Massai talks to Sebastian and happens to touch him, so that the boy has to seek escape under the steering-wheel. For that much „Indian" is simply too much. And if even the adults don´t want to get out of the car, these Massai can hardly be Winnetous!

The car turns into a gathering place for flies. Horrified remonstrance! „Close the doors and the windows or even more flies will come in, you´ll catch all kinds of diseases!" everybody screams. But the mosquitos are quicker and there´s a buzzing sound in the car as if it had turned into a helicopter about to take off. But instead of flying, the jeep drives off. The Massai watch it disappear as if it was a spaceship soaring to an unreachable world. What enormous distance 100 kilometres may be for people who have never seen any more than their own stretch of land and whose way of moving is the same as it was 100 years ago. But besides that, the Kenyan government doesn´t let the Massai go. For if the fauna is being exterminated by and by, then at least the Massai must be conserved as a tourist attraction.

In any case, the Massai didn´t give Bruno and the others the impression of being proud at all. Well, that´s the way it goes, when, over a span of 80 years, a country is first ravaged by slave traders, then by English colonists and now by tourists.

Before the first break, the last May-flies have been shooed away, which improves the general mood. So the trip to the village did pay off at last. One hour, says the driver. They take a look around.

„What, here, in the middle of nowhere?!" everybody cries out in unison.

„Hakuna matata!" the driver replies, locks up the jeep and disappears. So, out of necessity, they sit down and everybody orders something to drink.

One woman says: „Good God, they still eat with their hands!"

Everybody turns their eyes on a table where several black natives are having their meal. They are eating and chatting in quite a normal fashion, but for the eight passengers this is so unusual that they stare at them like at animals on a safari.

Bruno says: „I just can´t believe it!"

„What," somebody asks.

„That the Massai are still living today as in that village!"

Everybody nods in agreement.

That´s just the way it is, some people only believe what they see and others believe in something they cannot see and others still don´t believe even in the reality right in front of their eyes, and that´s what characterizes a run-of-the-mill tourist, and there really are masses of them.

A young man says: „I thought I had booked `A PLACE IN THE SUN´, actually, and this is what you get for your money! Something must have gone wrong with the reservation."

Bruno thinks: „Well, at least we have won `A PLACE IN THE SUN´."

An hour can be a long time, and everybody is happy that the ride continues. Again, there´s poverty on the streets.

„How much longer will it take till we arrive at last?" his wife asks sighing.

One can tell by the passengers´ faces that they will have to work hard in order to come to terms with what they have seen. But being in a paradisaical holiday resort, no paying tourist will be doing any work whatsoever for long and once more everything that had been announced in the brochures appears again: The Kenyan hotel parks on the Indian Ocean shore. At last there's food, fun and quiet and safe sleep.

Sunday. Bruno is a Catholic and belongs to the Christians who regularly go to church, that is, for Christmas and for Easter. When Bruno is told that there is a church near the hotel, he gets curious, since he has heard a lot about African services. So the Holbeins, along with three other hotel guests, take the opportunity to visit the morning service, accompanied by a hotel employee. But it's too far for them to walk there. For Bruno and the others are Germans after all, and they don't walk to church for miles and miles like the Kenyan natives do. Although miles and miles would be quite an exaggeration in this case. It's less than 2 kilometres from the hotel. The seven tourists squeeze themselves into a taxi. Shortly afterwards, they arrive in front of the church. Crowds of people are gathering. The building's construction is simplistic. The ringing of the church-bells is weaker than any jingling of a German village church. Bruno and the others take seat. On approximately 350 square yards, there are no less than 700 Catholics flocked together. They can't even close the church-door. For even outside there are natives queuing up, although it's neither Christmas nor Easter, but just an ordinary Sunday. The sermon begins. The priest is speaking loud and clear and uses his hands and arms to support his words. Compared to him, a German priest seems like a mere acolyte. Sebastian is getting bored. For, in spite of his IQ of 111,11, he doesn't understand one single word in Suaheli. The others don't understand a word either, but still they are impressed by the whole atmosphere. Actually, you don't need to understand much, since the sermon will be about God and all the rest anyway. The natives' singing makes the service more vivid and the power of their singing shows that they don't believe in a dead god. The church-choir makes any German church-choir seem like a bunch of absolute beginners. Then the crowd starts to move. Everybody claps their hands and sings. Then there's praying, preaching and more singing; and this goes on for one hour and a half. Probably the natives' enthusiasm with which they celebrate their service, has something to do with their ancestors and their former culture and religion. They probably haven't adopted their lively ways from the European missionairies, who possess as little enthusiasm as Franciscan monks. But don't worry, there will come a time when mission work will have converted even this kind of behaviour to death.

But what does that matter to Bruno? For he just wonders that there are so many believers. He had always thought that they were all heathens. He decides to make regular donations to the African Catholic Mission as soon as he gets home.

After church, the whites return to the hotel, for lunch. The natives just watch them leave, for their world is a different one.

Morning. It keeps raining softly even after beakfast. Bruno's family decides to go for a stroll in the shopping centre outside the protecting hotel walls. Not long ago, they drove through this small shopping centre with an old tractor that had been converted into a locomotive, the kind of which doesn't even exist as a trashy toy for children.

15 minutes later, they have reached their goal. The centre consists of 20 shops in one row 350 yards long. Native traders try to sell all kinds of tourist kitch to Bruno, Margot and Sebastian. Bruno may not know a lot about Kenya, but he does know that, as soon

as one engages in a deal, they won´t let go until one´s suitcase is filled with souvenirs.

There´s an Indian shop where there are fixed prices and where black native employees serve the customers at their Indian bosses´ command. Margot sees a golden pendant in the shape of Africa, which she had already noticed on other tourists´ necks. The wallet is drawn and Margot is the proud owner of Golden Africa, which she instantly hangs around her neck.

It´s still raining softly. That´s a good opportunity to have a drink. The three decide to order something in a small African restaurant. But, good God, Bruno has too little money left and he only realizes it after everything has been ordered. He can already see himself being accused of bilking. The waiter arrives. Bruno flushes. He tries to explain to him that he has only half of the bill´s worth with him. The waiter doesn´t understand where the problem is. So Bruno repeats that his money isn´t enough to pay the bill. Now something unbelievable happens! The waiter looks at him calmly and replies: „Hakuna matata! You can pay some other time. Would you like something to eat, too?“

They cannot believe their ears and order three sandwiches. That´s just how it is, in Germany you don´t trust a black person an inch, just as a supermarket employee won´t trust a regular customer over a sum of 1 cent; Bruno is met with more confidence here, than he would put in a close acquaintance.

It stops raining and the three Holbeins return to the hotel where trust is as large as every single guest´s wallet.

It´s the second day of the second week. Yesterday Bruno and his family met a Swiss married couple. They have a daughter who is the same age as Sebastian. The children liked each other immediately. The adults first had to smell carefully at one another, as it were, but as is typical for holidays, you get quickly acquainted and start to make plans for joint activities, since they will be here for just 8 more days and they must experience something during that time.

Bruno makes a discovery. Most Swiss are a league of their own. If you know the Suabians and thought that their diligence and thrift were unique, you either don´t know any Swiss persons or too few of them. If you ask a Swiss about his profession, it may well occur that he won´t finish talking. For work and material things are more important to this nation of 4 millions, than his own little house is to a Suabian.

How lucky Bruno is to have won a free flight to Kenya, or else, who knows, he would never have come into close contact with Swiss people. Although, in theory, Swiss people may also be met in Italy. For they have a third less free time than Germans have and often belong to the category of „in-and-out" tourists. Into the aeroplane and out again. Snapshots of the hotel, the sun, the beach, the swimming-pool and before returning home again, they have to ride in a taxi at least once. For you have to see something of the country and the inhabitants after all. This will be repeated 2 to 3 times a year. So these run-of-the-mill tourists, who certainly are not exclusively from Switzerland, get around a lot without, however, seeing or understanding anything about the countries visited.

Today the taxi-ride is on. And off they go to Mombasa. The driver steps on it as if the taxman were after him. Then the ghettos and the poverty appear again and, would you believe it, it´s a miracle. For reportedly, 1. seeing is believing, 2. many a blind man was cured by a miracle, 3. Bruno is beginning to see again. For he is no longer turning a blind eye on Mombasa and the poverty in particular.

However, there isn´t too much to see in Mombasa apart from the catastrophic traffic, which in itself may be considered a tourist attraction. The traffic rages as it would in the Berlin rush-hour, if every traffic-light was out of order. Bruno is quite surprised that there is not a single accident to take a picture of.

Then they arrive at Mombasa´s old port. Everybody gets out of the car. The children are fascinated as they watch the cargo ships that are just being unloaded by workers in miserable clothes. Compared to this toiling, any German construction worker seems like a civil servant of the clerical class. The children take in everything and the adults take photographs as if they got 1,000 DM per picture.

The ride goes on. There are men dragging empty to overloaded wooden carts on the streets of Mombasa. A tough job just for a couple of cents.

Then they halt. Now it´s time to visit the wood carvers. Shaded by wooden huts, more than 1,000 (one thousand) workers in - how could it be otherwise - miserable clothes, with no shoes and with no occupational safety whatsoever, are carving souvenirs by the piece. The only occupational safety are their nimble and skilful hands. These working conditions would spread fear among 99.9% of the German employed, unemployed and trade unionists and would make employers regain their faith in a god named „EXPLOITER".

After Bruno and the other´s stunned gaze and overwhelming impressions, the ride goes on. Bruno often sees children shining shoes or carrying heavy loads in order to contribute to their family´s subsistence (or survival?).

The next stop is at a jeweller´s shop. They look at the jewellery and every single family buys rings and chains only tourists or people from India can afford. For this shop, like most shops, is owned by Indian people.

In Kenya, the Indians are a distinguished community with their own culture. Apart from the Europeans, they own most of the capital and often treat the black population the way the English colonists have not so long ago. If the Indian were worth as much in India as here, India would be wealthier than Germany.

At this point it should be noted that even Bruno realizes that, if race riots should break out some day, which isn´t unlikely considering the prevailing poverty, the black population will first take their revenge on the Indian people before they take the Europeans to task.

The ride leads back to the hotel where the black natives take care of the tourists like of the English colonists 50 years ago, and isn´t that remarkable, even Bruno got that in the meantime.

There are various kinds of tourists. One of these types is the pig-tourist, who Bruno, along with the Swiss acquaintance, gets to know at a bar, after the wives and kids have gone to bed. Loud music is ringing in their ears. An unknown German talks to Bruno: „You still got to choose one, too, huh?“

Bruno casually answers: „Yes, I´m trying to make my mind up what to drink“.

The stranger sneers: „Man, I meant something to fuck!“

To which the Swiss replies: „No, we don´t need that, we got our wives at the hotel“

The stranger: „Jeez, you´re kidding!“

Bruno cannot believe that he has come upon a brothel, but how should he know that almost any bar or discotheque in Kenya is a brothel? Certainly not from the glossy brochures. Only now does Bruno notice the numerous black women sitting at the bar or at the tables who are waiting for their customers or who have already become the victim of a tourist. Bruno turns to the stranger and asks: „Don´t you think that you are exploiting the poverty of the women here?"

„Oh, come on, you don´t have a clue. Without us they would be starving, just think about it, a whore gets as much for a good fuck as a worker will earn in 2-3 weeks, and sometimes 2-3 whores are fucked at a time and so several earn from just one guy a night".

The rest of the conversation is not worth mentioning, unless one wishes to lower oneself onto the level of a sex-tourist. In any case, the stranger seems to think actually that he is a missionary. For religious missionaries say: „I give you bread and you worship my god". And sex-tourists say: „You worship my dick and I give you money".

Without paying further attention to the stranger, both finish their drinks and go back to the hotel.

On the penultimate day of „A PLACE IN THE SUN", Bruno-Columbus comes alive. However, without muskets and cannons. Wearing a safari suit and loaded with photographic equipment, he decides to take a taxi to a near village. He leaves the choice of the village to the driver. For Bruno is determined to take a closer look behind the hotel walls. He is, however, all by himself, since the other adventurers prefer to go on discovering the hotel, the beach, the swimming-pool and the sun-beams.

The taxi-ride ends after a mere 5 minutes. Roads that are muddy from the rain lead to miserable huts, which Bruno had only known from TV until now. On TV, however, an adventure is quite different from the harsh reality Bruno now finds himself in. The villagers´ shelters mostly lack electricity and running water, though there actually is running water which is, however, not piped to taps but due to the masses of rain that make life in the huts nearly unbearable. The cooking is done at a small fire-place in the hut offering the inhabitants, who have to live one top of one another, only damp ground to sleep and sit on. And would you believe, Bruno leaves his camera in his pocket and hits upon the idea that the villagers might not feel like being photographed like monkeys on safaris. At least, Bruno has more decency than Columbus ever had. Poor children surround him and beg for some money or for sweets. An adult approaches him and wants to sell some corn, it seems to be the only thing he can spare. Bruno finds it strange that 1. any paying tourist may fly to the remotest regions of the world, 2. that fruit, coffee, tea and what not is exported from the farest corners of the third world and 3. that it doesn´t seem humanly possible to transport surplus food of rich countries to starving children and adults. Instead, corrupt politicians are given millions and millions for development aid, of which the starving majority of this world and of this village get as little as of the surplus food of the hotel buffets.

As Bruno is sitting in the taxi again, he hands banknotes to one or the other before leaving, for what else is he supposed to do right now?

Shortly afterwards, he is back at the beach and recovers from his impressions.

On the last day before the return flight, Bruno is busy packing his suitcase and dealing with the customs formalities. Then tips are distributed to the staff; then he turns, like many other guests, too, into a good Samaritan and gives away clothes and shoes worn out by Margot, Sebastian and himself, that in Germany wouldn´t even be worthy of a welfare recipient.

In the evening, Bruno goes to bed with a clear conscience.

4 o´clock in the morning. The alarm-clock makes a noise and three sleepy figures tumble out of their beds. Shortly afterwards, some staff member knocks on the door to make sure that the Holbeins are awake. After all, „A PLACE IN THE SUN" only paid for two weeks and then, why would you want to keep tourists when they have already been stripped of their money?

5 a.m.. After breakfast, Bruno and his family as well as 20 other tourists are sitting in the shuttle-bus. They are heading for the airport. Bruno sleeps while Mombasa presents its quiet side. Few people are scattered on the streets. Traffic is flowing along quietly like in a little drowsy town in Germany. But poverty is haunting Mombasa just as the new poverty is haunting Germany.

After arriving at the airport, they have to find the right luggage buried in a heap of hundreds of suitcases along with masses of tangled-up people. Porters are waiting to apply their working capacities in exchange for a tip. Before the Holbeins can say Jack Robinson, three porters are standing by each one holding a suitcase, which costs Bruno his very last dime.

Then they have to suffer the same procedure as on the outward flight. So far, everything has been overcome. Two hours to go before the departure. Bruno, like thousands of other people, uses the remaining time for tax-free shopping, which ultimately terminates the holiday budget.

Flights to every country under the sun are being called. Then, at last, so is the flight „Mombasa-Frankfurt", and it takes off according to schedule, too. By the time the hostesses explain what is to be done in the event of events, Bruno is so excited that he has forgotten his fear of flying. This much is certain, however: if the plane should crash, Bruno at least will die relaxed and stress-free, though, shortly before the impact, stress will probably increase to a maximum and relaxation will decrease to zero.

He´ll need 8 hours and 10 minutes of endurance!

Chapter 3

3 BACK

Phew, Bruno takes a deep breath again. Landing passed off amid the passengers´ applause, without incident. Barely has the captain been congratulated for the safe flight home, when the pushing and shoving at the exit door begins. Yes indeed, this is Germany´s famous jostling and hurrying! As soon as the passengers arrive at the passport control, there doesn´t seem to be much left of Kenya´s „polepole". Because the clearance, how should it be otherwise, has to be done quickly and impersonally, which is annoying.

But then suddenly, Bruno gasps for breath. Hastily he searches for his passport. While doing this, he gets more and more aware of his sun-tan and it frightens him. For his skin has got so dark, that he can almost picture himself filling out an asylum application form. But how could it be different? The little red book, the contents of which don´t require much education to read, appears shortly before he gets to stand in front of the customs officer. And there´s one thing Bruno is sure of, this has spared him a lot of red tapery.

„No!" somebody queuing in front of the Holbeins answers when the female customs officer asks whether there is anything to declare.
„Do you have live animals with you?"
Still in a holiday mood, the next answer follows: „No, we left our cat at the animal home!"
A strained smile flies over the officer´s lips, then it´s Bruno and his family´s turn.
„Have you got anything to declare?"
„No!"
„Do you have live animals with you?"

„No!"
Then they enter the tangle of people again.

At the parking lot, Bruno and the others notice that their summer clothes are as appropriate for a temperature of 5°C as a thick fur coat in Kenya.
Not long afterwards, Bruno is driving his BMW on the motorway which is resembling the Hockenheim racetrack. As if driving fast, faster, fastest could prolong a lifetime or increase the distance to heaven. Everything is quiet now. Sebastian is sleeping and Margot is dozing. Bruno imagines a Kenyan actually winning a free flight to Germany for two weeks. For there might as well be a lottery in Kenya called „A PLACE IN THE COLD".

So the lucky guy would fly over here and ride over the German motorways and country roads by taxi, and he would watch the life of the inhabitants through the windscreen, stay at a five-star hotel where he would have a greater time than God in his heavenly paradise, then he would join sightseeing tours through cities reading everything of interest in glossy brochures, and after two weeks´ time, he would fly back home. There he would tell everyone who would listen, or would not, how great his free flight to „A PLACE IN THE COLD" was and how great life in Germany is. In this way, an equally abstract work of art would form as when a run-of-the-mill tourist praises the great hotel conveniences in a third-world country.

At home, the suitcases are quickly dragged from the boot into the corridor. Shortly afterwards, Sebastian goes to bed exhausted. Before his parents do as he does, they switch on the TV-set for the 8 o´clock news. For one might have missed out on something in the meantime. But, little wonder, everything has stayed the same, there´s not even a bloody sensation which might enliven the latest news, but just the same babbling as there was 2 weeks ago.

Had it been 2 years, then there wouldn't be any more news than in a developing country such as Kenya. This is the kind of homely conservative life that immediately makes Bruno feel so good again!

Soon the night is over and Sunday doesn't begin before noon. Getting up, Bruno and Margot feel that they didn't quite survive the flight undamaged, for all the sitting around has made their muscles and their joints as ponderous as a conservative structure. While they unpack their suitcases, they can feel every single movement. But it has to be done, as the Polish charwoman will be here tomorrow, and so the dirty laundry has to be arranged for her, provided that clothes of every colour cast on a heap may be called an arrangement. But why bother, in the end it's the staff who is in charge of the dirty work.

Lunchtime. The microwave prepares a pre-cooked meal that would be an insult to any menu at McDonald's. But it's better to cook badly at home than to go out to have an even worse meal.

Then a few telephone calls have to be done. For Bruno and the others have a lot to tell about Kenya, the hotel, the sun and the beach.

But in spite of what he has to say, Bruno cannot see the light, but at least he can see a small speck of light somewhere in the distance, no bigger than a flickering star in the night sky, shifting Bruno's life into a different perspective. And at last, Bruno sees a tiny flame and he realizes that the prize of „A PLACE IN THE SUN" finally did bring about something positive: He got to see and experience something different from the usual, from the same daily way to work, the same leisure activities, the same hotel at the same beach every year; and then he catches his opinions about the world and about life through television, radio and newspapers - opinions that mean as much as promises in election campaigns! Yes, that´s what responsible citizens are made of.

But Bruno remains loyal to the facts of life and wistfully arranges, before going to sleep, his suit, shirt, tie and briefcase, for tomorrow will be Monday, and then duty will be duty and thoughts will be thoughts.